Rachel

CERTIFICATE OF

FREEDOM

LYNNE KOSITSKY

RACHEL
CERTIFICATE OF
FREEDOM
LYNNE KOSITSKY

PENGUIN
CANADA

PENGUIN CANADA

Penguin Group (Canada), a division of Pearson Penguin Canada Inc.,
10 Alcorn Avenue, Toronto, Ontario M4V 3B2

Penguin Group (U.K.), 80 Strand, London WC2R 0RL, England
Penguin Group (U.S.), 375 Hudson Street, New York, New York 10014, U.S.A.
Penguin Group (Australia) Inc., 250 Camberwell Road, Camberwell, Victoria 3124, Australia
Penguin Group (Ireland), 25 St. Stephen's Green, Dublin 2, Ireland
Penguin Books India (P) Ltd, 11, Community Centre, Panchsheel Park, New Delhi – 110 017, India
Penguin Group (New Zealand), cnr Rosedale and Airborne Roads, Albany, Auckland 1310,
New Zealand
Penguin Books (South Africa) (Pty) Ltd, 24 Sturdee Avenue, Rosebank 2196, South Africa

Penguin Group, Registered Offices: 80 Strand, London WC2R 0RL, England

First published 2003

1 2 3 4 5 6 7 8 9 10   (WEB)

Copyright © Lynne Kositsky, 2003
Cover and interior illustrations © Ron Lightburn, 2003
Chapter opener illustrations © Ron Lightburn, 2003
Design: Matthews Communications Design Inc.
Map © Sharon Matthews

Manufactured in Canada.

NATIONAL LIBRARY OF CANADA CATALOGUING IN PUBLICATION

Kositsky, Lynne, 1947–
Rachel : certificate of freedom / Lynne Kositsky.

(Our Canadian girl)
ISBN 0-14-301462-5

1. Black Canadians—Nova Scotia—Shelbourne—History—18th
century—Juvenile fiction. 2. Freedmen—Nova Scotia—Juvenile fiction.
3. Slavery—Nova Scotia—Juvenile fiction. I. Title. II. Title: Certificate of freedom. III. Series.

PS8571.O85R34 2003   jC813'.54   C2003-902889-5
PZ7

Visit the Penguin Group (Canada) website at **www.penguin.ca**

For Michael,
through thick and thin

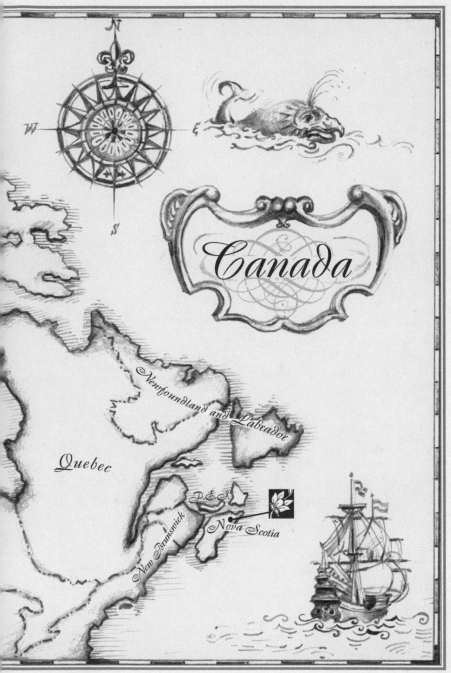

Canada

Newfoundland and Labrador

Quebec

P.E.I.

New Brunswick

Nova Scotia

 Marks the location of the story

RACHEL'S STORY CONTINUES

I N 1783, Britain lost the Revolutionary War against the American colonies and began to move Loyalists, including black former slaves, up to its remaining colonies, now part of Canada. Many of the black Loyalists were sent from New York to Nova Scotia.

Rachel Sparrow, her mother Sukey, and her stepfather Titan all moved to a small black settlement, Birchtown, where they were forced to live in a pit-cabin for their first winter, an intensely cold season almost unknown in those parts. Rachel's brother Jem was born around Christmas, rations were poor, and the pit-cabin was mercilessly cold and crowded.

Titan managed to earn some money as a skilled carpenter, and in the spring of 1784, when it became evident that the family was not going to get the land promised by the British government, Titan decided to move his family to Shelburne, a mostly white town further to the east. Shelburne was booming. The land was more fertile, and the opportunities for work better, as there were many new houses to erect for the white population. Titan built a house of his own in the small black area of town, and the family settled there.

But the atmosphere in Shelburne became increasingly intolerant, as de-listed white soldiers, unable to find work, blamed the black population for accepting jobs at cheaper rates. In the summer of 1784 they staged a riot, pulling down all the black houses, and Rachel and her family had to escape, moving with great sorrow back to their first home, the pit-cabin, in Birchtown.

Now it is late summer, and, despite the setbacks, Rachel has high hopes for her future. After all, she's made a good start on learning to read and write. But life has another lesson in store for her—one that will teach her just how precious her freedom really is.

New York, *October* 1783.

THIS is to certify to whoever it may concern that the Bearer hereof

Rachel

a Negro, resorted to the British Lines in consequence of Proclamations of Sir William Howe, and Sir Henry Clinton, late Commanders in Chief in America; and that the said Negro has hereby his Excellency Sir Guy Carleton's Permission to go to Nova-Scotia, or wherever else *she* may think proper.

By order of Brigadier General Birch.

CHAPTER № 1

Rachel's stepdaddy, Titan, was building a new house for the family down by the shore. He'd been doing a deal of work for the most important man in Birchtown, Colonel Blucke, mending and making, and in return the Colonel had lent him some tools for his own private use. Titan had been busy, and Rachel loved to go down and see how the house was growing, like a fat, square August flower blooming out of the earth. It took her mind off other things, like Mamma's uncertain temper and the rotten, musty smell of where they lived now.

"You're doing fine, Titan," she said. "It's not as good as our Maybe House, but it's a heap better than the pit-cabin. When d'you reckon it'll be finished?"

"Just one log on another till the job be done," replied Titan, who never talked much.

"By fall, maybe? I'd hate to spend another winter in the pit." She shuddered as she remembered the previous winter. It had been cramped and freezing cold. "I could help," she went on. "I'd love to. I've done all my chores for the day, and my reading practice."

Nathan Crowley, the white boy who'd taught her to read, didn't come to Birchtown often now. It was too dangerous. The place was a buzzing wasp's nest of Negroes angry at the whites who'd thrown them out of Shelburne and whites angry at the Negroes for being in Nova Scotia at all. These white men came from Shelburne every now and then to jeer at the Negro folk and make trouble. It had become a kind of pastime, like going to the fair. There was little enough paid work, so they had scant else to do.

Rachel got down on her knees and held a log steady so Titan could saw it in half. "Thank goodness for trees." She smiled. "They're like enormous people with arms outstretched, aiming to protect us."

"You imaginin' again?" Mamma, baby Jem under her arm, had come down from the pit-cabin. "I jus' taking this child over to Nanna Jacklin's. Then you an' me goin' berry pickin', girl." Mamma pronounced it "*betty* pickin'."

Rachel stood up and slung her hands along her hips. Mamma was always wishing her somewhere else just when she was getting comfortable. In fact, truth be told, Mamma could be the worst kind of nuisance, always arranging Rachel and what she was doing.

She scowled at her mother. "I'm already helping here."

"You comin' with me. I need a mess of fruit and then mebbe I make a pie wi' some kin' of cornmeal crust. Titan love them pies in summer. Ain't that so, Titan?"

Titan flicked away a fly and wiped the sweat off his forehead. He went at the wood some more as though Mamma hadn't spoken, his face carved into downward lines, his lips a tight knot of concentration. The saw was none too sharp and he was having trouble making the first cut. Unwilling to behave for him, the log swung out sideways.

"See? I told you he needs me," said Rachel. She helped Titan rearrange the log.

But Mamma was already marching along the path to Nanna Jacklin's, her shoulders up and huffy, her back straight as a ramrod. "I need you more, girl. Time you listen some. You can't tell the deep of the well by the size of the bucket."

Mamma's sayings often didn't hold any sense at all for Rachel. She made a monster face and stuck her tongue out at Mamma's retreating back. But all the same, Titan was giving her one of his quick, curt nods, meaning she should go, and she knew when she was beaten. She took off after Mamma, her neck clammy, her skirt sticking to her legs in the heat. At least she'd be able to eat some of those berries, grown big on sun and summer. They needn't all be kept for the pie. Even now she could almost savour the explosion of sweet, tart flavour on her tongue.

CHAPTER N° 2

It was cooler in the deep summer woods,
and Rachel was suddenly glad she'd come.
Though they'd eaten dried cranberries whenever
they could get them last winter, she and Mamma
were in the wrong area for them now. The sour
fruit liked boggy land that sucked Rachel's feet
down into it, and besides, cranberries hadn't come
ripe yet. Rachel's Indian friend Ann-Marie, who
knew much about the ways of wild things, had
once told her that they needed the first kiss of
frost on them. Judging by the weather, that likely
wouldn't happen for a while.

Mamma, who couldn't get her tongue around the sound of them either, called them *cranbetties*. "Sure would love some o' them cranbetties," she'd say when they'd had nothing to eat but cornmeal for days. The word was contagious. After a while, everyone in the family called them *cranbetties* and looked forward to eating them again.

Though there were no *cranbetties,* there were *raspbetties* and *blackbetties* scattered through the forest, their dense, leafy bushes intertwined with other vines and plants. Some of the blackberries were still greenish white, unready to pick, and they resisted anyhow, clinging to their brambly branches as if loath to leave home.

Their shape and colour reminded Rachel of the missus's pale thimble on the plantation long, long ago, and she shivered. For a moment she could see the missus's white hand as it moved up and down, up and down, sewing a fine, even seam. Since it was the same hand that had often pulled her hair or slapped her face, it was the last thing she cared to think about. Instead she blotted out the memory by working hard, seeking and picking. The ripe berries fell off as soon as she touched them and dropped into her skirt. Too many went by a side road into her mouth, but she just couldn't resist them.

"Don't you eat all them blackbetties, missy," said Mamma, who must have seen the telltale stains on Rachel's lips and teeth. "They for the pie."

"No, Mamma. Yes, Mamma." Rachel swallowed quickly. Mamma went back to filling her little basket, which she'd made herself in the old African way.

Low, brittle bushes with a special kind of round fruit grew among the rocks under the trees. Rachel bent to pick. The tiny berries, which she'd tasted before, were sweet as honey, and as she dropped them into her skirt they made a greyish stain.

"Don't be pickin' *them*." Mamma drew back, fearful.

"They're fine, Mamma. Ann-Marie told me."

"We ain't pickin' nothin' I never seen before. And besides, they *blue*. No nat'ral food blue. *Blue* for the sky, say the good Lord. Blue for the wide ocean."

Rachel sighed. "They're bluebetties, Mamma. *Blue berries*. They're supposed to be eaten. That's if the squirrels don't get them first."

Mamma looked a mite doubtful. She picked one up, sniffed it, and tasted it with the edge of her tongue. "Bluebetties? They the same colour as Jem's eyes when he new hatched."

"And they're delicious. Eat one."

A slight sound, a *crunch,* behind the trees—a bird maybe, or one of those ornery squirrels. But the air seemed suddenly darker, the lacy patches of sunlight gone. As Rachel turned towards the noise she caught a quick flash of red. It wasn't a cardinal or robin, or any sort of small creature. Too big. Too heavy. Twigs cracked. She started, and as she grabbed Mamma's elbow, a few berries tumbled from her skirt.

"Clumsy girl," grumbled Mamma. "All 'em ripe betties, gone for nothin'."

"No, not for nothing. Mamma, there's someone in the woods here. I'm sure of it."

"There you go, always imaginin'. What a chore it is to have an imaginin' child." But now Mamma caught sight of something too, a way off behind a tree, a large something. Could have been a bear, except for the colour.

"It looks like a soldier's jacket," whispered Rachel. "A redcoat."

"We goin' home," Mamma said firmly, the small scar on her forehead blazing. Rachel was terrified when Mamma's scar stood out like a careless lick of crimson paint. It was akin to the weather vane on Colonel Blucke's roof spinning round and round—told of bad storms coming. A knot of hair fell forward, covering Mamma's forehead.

They were scurrying through the woods now, towards the Birchtown settlement, as fast as their bare feet would cover the stony earth. Berries cascaded from Rachel's skirt. They were spilling from Mamma's basket, too, which she carried on her head. But neither Rachel nor Mamma cared a whit. White men were dangerous. They had pulled down the Maybe House in Shelburne with ship's tackle. They had bothered the Nigra folk of Birchtown time and time again, cat-calling, messing in their business, pitching stones.

The only white person that Rachel had any trust in was Nathan Crowley, and he was just a boy. Still, she wished he were with them now. If nothing else, he could make fearsome faces. When he pulled down the corners of his eyes and stuck fingers up both nostrils, he could frighten the local dogs away. She wasn't sure if he could frighten actual people.

"Stop." A man stepped in front of them, holding up his hand. How he'd got there before them was anyone's guess. He must have moved fast, fast, through the trees and run down the hill on the other side. His ginger moustache bristled. His yellow hair and pink, pockmarked face glimmered in the dusky light. Rachel was sure she'd seen him before, but her heart was beating so fast she couldn't remember where, couldn't recall anything, in fact, not even her own name.

"Nigras, good afternoon," he said, kindly enough. "I'm here in the King's employment."

That made Rachel even more frightened, for he didn't look as though he could possibly be in the King's employment, or anyone else's. His red jacket was filthy and threadbare, his boots scuffed and muddy. He hadn't seen the inside of an army barracks for months, was clear as water one of the many de-listed soldiers scavenging around the area. Besides, what would the King, way over in a foreign country and sitting in his palace eating pudding with cream, want with two shabby Nigra folk? Rachel couldn't imagine.

"What you wantin', suh?" asked Mamma, polite as she knew how to be. It made no sense being rude to white folk, especially when they carried long, sharp-nosed guns tucked into their waistbands. They could crush you fast as spit at you. Whisking her basket down and setting it on the grass before her, brushing her hair back off her scar, Mamma stood, arms folded, waiting.

"His Majesty has charged me to examine the Nigras hereabout, make sure they're all truly free."

"Oh, we free, sir. We truly free. We been put down in the book of Nigras, and we got our ce'ticates to prove it." Mamma couldn't say *certificates,* still had the sounds of Africa in her mouth.

"Certificates of freedom?"

"Yessuh," nodded Mamma, her bottom lip catching between her teeth.

Rachel thought hard. At first she couldn't recall the certificates of freedom. What were they? Where had they come from? Who had given them to her and Mamma? It was all lost in the fearful fog of the past.

"We given 'em in New York, before we get on the ship," Mamma went on, as if reading Rachel's thoughts. "Them white men ask us, did we help the army of King George? And we say yessuh.

Then they say, 'You free. We take care of you. You never need go back be slaves.'"

All at once, Rachel remembered. It had been a dark little room near the wharf in New York, with cracked walls and spiderwebs, smelling of mould and salt. An important-looking soldier with shiny buttons was sitting at a packing case for a desk, filling in names on sheets of printed paper. Some people, like her and Mamma, were lucky. They got the precious certificates and hugged them close as treasure maps. But a few were refused. One young girl lunged behind the desk of the gold-button soldier, throwing her arms like tangled ropes around his knees. She begged and cried, she banged her head against the floor, but it made no difference. Her massa was waiting outside, ready to carry her back to the plantation. There she was in a trice, all her freedom poured out of her, a slave again. Rachel blinked as though smacked. Where was that girl now? What had happened to her?

"I need to see those certificates," the man with the ginger moustache declared, bringing her back to the present. "King George needs the proof that you're truly free, d'you see?"

"Yessuh," Mamma murmured. A grasshopper skimmed out of a bush and landed on the man's boot.

"Well, where are they? I got better things to do than stand around passing the time of day with you lazy Nigras. The King's business is mighty important." With the heel of his other boot he squashed the grasshopper. It left a nasty brown smear on his instep.

There is something in his voice, Rachel thought, *something ugly and familiar.* But she still couldn't remember where she'd seen him before. Trembling, she stared down at her bare feet, which were dusty and calloused, before glancing at Mamma again. She was praying Mamma had the certificates with her. She could show them to the man, he would go away, and, apart from a few spilled berries, all would be right again.

"They in my skirt. I sew 'em ce'ticates tight in my skirt to keep 'em safe." Mamma started picking at her hem with her berry-stained fingers, but the white stitches were stout and resisted pulling. The man took a fast step towards her and pulled out a knife. Rachel gasped. Tears spattered down Mamma's face like raindrops.

"Steady," he grinned. "I'm just going to slit those stitches." As he slid the knife along the dark edge of Mamma's skirt, a small bundle of folded papers, dirty and tattered, fell out. Locked inside her hem for almost a year, they'd been dipped in rain, snow, dust, and mud, as her long skirt had trailed across the landscape.

"What's the names on these here certificates?" he demanded, without trying to decipher them. "They're faded."

"Rachel and Sukey," whispered Rachel, realizing with a shock that he couldn't read.

"Rachel and Sukey, eh? That you? And you?"

"Yessuh," they replied in unison.

"These look to be in order, but I must show

them to my officer. Come along with me. Forget the basket," he growled as Mamma bent to pick it up. "There'll be plenty of time for that later."

He gave Mamma a sharp nudge, but she managed to keep her balance. Throwing her arm around Rachel, she gave her a tight hug, and they began, all three of them, to trudge along the twilight path towards Shelburne.

With a flick of his hand, the man crammed the certificates into the pouch that served as the back pocket of his britches. Or at least Rachel thought he did. His fingers moved so slickly, and dusk was falling so fast, she couldn't be sure.

CHAPTER N.º 3

A big bubble was rising in Rachel's throat, a sour bubble of fear. It came up from her supperless stomach, almost choking her.

The man had marched them straight past Shelburne, that white folks town, where you might expect his commanding officer to be. "Not here, not here," he chided them when they tried to slow down. "It's a ways further on."

Now they were trekking through unfamiliar country, as the darkest shades of evening began to lower across the land. It was a moonless night with just the faintest flicker of stars. Scissor-like twigs sprang out of nowhere to catch them in the face. Brambles pinched and scratched their legs. But worst of all, they could hear the beasts howling eerily in the forest. *Wolves and bears,* thought Rachel with terror, *maybe a lynx.* This was *their* place, animal town. They didn't need a survey map, like human folk, to tell them where to live. They went wherever they wanted. They ate what they could kill. It just didn't do to be out after dark, and for the first time Rachel prayed that the white man knew how to use his gun.

Mamma was moaning, "I need to get back to my Jem. I can't be travellin' the wild woods all night. My bebby needs feedin'."

"Not long now. Stop yer crabbing."

Mamma and Rachel were stumbling along, exhausted and frightened. *This was almost as bad as the war,* thought Rachel, *when you never knew who was going to come out from behind the bushes and aim a gun at you, and you never knew what side folk were on when you came face to face with them. Friend or foe?* she wanted to yell at the man.

19

Friend or foe? But when he came close she could smell the liquor and sharp, angry sweat on him, so she figured she already knew.

A house loomed out of the blackness. Just one candle glimmered in a window, throwing a puddle of dim light into the gloom.

"This is the first place we need to stop," said the man, though it was a strange time to go calling.

"Firs' place?" asked Mamma. "How many we need to show our ce'ticates to 'fore we can go home?"

He didn't answer her.

Now the beginnings of remembering were stirring in Rachel's brain. Her last meeting with this man had been something to do with tuppence, with spending money that Titan had given her, and that meeting had been very nasty indeed. Suddenly, the memory emerged, wormy and disgusting, like a fat white maggot crawling out of a barrel of flour. She tried to lose the recollection again out of sheer fright, push it back into her brain, but it wouldn't go. It was too horribly clear, like an ancestor portrait hanging on one of the missus's walls in South Carolina.

The soldier standing in front of her was one of the two men who'd stopped her on her way to the white people store in summer. *Oh, no,* she thought.

"Tell your daddy," he'd said after quizzing her that day, "tell your daddy from us that he's taking work away from respectable white folk, men who are starving on the streets. Got that?"

"Yessuh," she'd whimpered.

"Then don't you forget it, Nigra. We lost the war for *you*." He'd shaken her till she fell. Stumbling up, she'd run home as fast as her legs would carry her.

She wished she could dash home now. She wished she could signal Mamma, tell her what was wrong so they could both get going, but the man had his eyes on them every single second. And there was still that pistol in his waistband. What did he want with them? Why were they here? It was nothing to do with certificates, she was sure as sugar of that.

"Ho there, George," cried the man, knocking on the door of the house but still glaring at Rachel and Mamma. "Come down now."

"Go away," came a voice from inside. "It's the middle of the night. Respectable folk are all at home abed . . . like I was till you came a-bothering me."

"George, it's your own dear brother, Serjeant Gyssop. And I've something special to show 'ee."

Rachel and Mamma clung together. Rachel thought she never wanted to catch sight of George Gyssop, he had such a wretched, gruff voice, and one nasty man, the one they had in front of them, was just about enough for anybody. In any case, there was silence. The door stayed firmly shut.

"What all this got to do with ce'ticates?" asked Mamma, her voice as thin as whey.

Serjeant Gyssop, the fellow in the red coat they'd been trudging through the night with, ignored her. "Come on, George," he cried. "You won't be sorry for it, I promise."

Silence again. Then the rattle of a doorknob. The squeak of a latch going up. A creak as the door opened. Someone peered through it, a nightcap on, with a few sparse red hairs sticking out around it. George Gyssop blinked into the darkness.

"What's all this? What's all this, hey? Serjeant, you'll be the death of me."

"See these here? Two fine Nigra slaves. And one of 'em's for 'ee."

Rachel gasped.

"We ain't slaves!" shouted Mamma. "We free Nigras. You got our ce'ticates in you back pocket, you divil."

Serjeant Gyssop bared his teeth and shook his fist at her. Mamma shut up fast.

"Don't know what she's talking about, George. I got these two off a slave trader down south a ways in one of the lost colonies. I'm aiming to give you the older one in settlement of my debts. A stout wench she is, too."

"Well . . ." mused George, "I was wanting help. And you do owe me a king's ransom, Serjeant, it's true." He paused a moment. "And I'll never see any penny of ought you owe me if I'm any judge of character. You're just like our daddy. Can't keep a shilling to your name. So I might as well take the older wench. What d'you aim to do with the younger?"

"Never you mind, brother. I got a place for her further along the road a ways."

Both Rachel and Mamma were sobbing now. Rachel couldn't believe the trap they'd tumbled into. And to be separated from Mamma. How could she bear it?

"Look in your brother's pouch, Massa Gyssop," she cried through her tears. "Our certificates of freedom are there. We're free Nigras, freed by General Birch himself for helping in the war. We're nobody's slaves."

Serjeant smiled. Casually he untied the pouch and shook the contents onto the ground. Out fell three pennies, a brass button, and a greening crust of bread.

"They were there, they *were!*" Rachel yelled. "He's done away with them somehow."

"He jus' throw them on the earth for the wild beasts to tear 'part," howled Mamma.

"You know how it is with Nigras," Serjeant muttered to his brother. "They'll try anything to tie knots in the truth. These here are slaves, fresh from the fields. I got them fair and square."

"And how was that, Serjeant? You with no money to speak of?"

"I won them in a card game, deuces wild."

"And they say no good can come of gambling. Ha!" George Gyssop stood outside his door pondering as the dawn birds began to sing and the sky patched pink in the east. He stared up and down the woodland path a few times, as if to make sure no one was coming, then grinned, wide and deep, showing a row of blackened teeth.

"Right you are, Serjeant," he said, winking. "I'll take your word for it. Give me the woman. She looks like she might do a decent day's work when she stops snivelling."

"You won't regret it, George. And now we're quits."

The two men pulled Rachel and Mamma, who were holding fast to each other, apart. Last thing Rachel saw through her rainy eyes was Mamma being dragged inside the house.

"No, no," Mamma wailed, her voice cracked as an old crow's. "My Rachel. My bebby. My Titan. You ain't goin' to take me 'way from them. You can't!" As she disappeared, the door closed with a bang. The latch thumped down. The brass door-knob turned.

Then Serjeant Gyssop picked up the pennies and the button and stuffed them in his pouch. Kicking the bread into the grass, he pulled his gun from his waistband, trained it on Rachel, and told her to get moving.

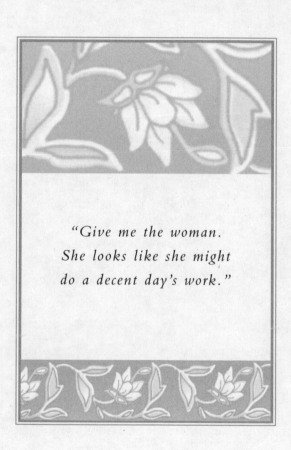

*"Give me the woman.
She looks like she might
do a decent day's work."*

They went around and around, up and down, off the path and back onto it. Rachel was sure Serjeant Gyssop was trying to confuse her so she wouldn't know where Mamma was. And she was mighty confused. The sun, after its first shell-pink patchiness, had totally hidden its face, so she couldn't even tell which way they were headed. Though Mamma had a strong sense of direction, she had none. It was still early, the day unripe and misty, and they met not a soul on their travels.

Finally they reached the outskirts of a small town. It looked unfamiliar, but could it be

Shelburne, come upon from the other side? Rachel hadn't a clue. All she knew was that it had started to rain a good half hour back, and she was soaked to the skin. Her bare feet were freezing, and bleeding from the many sharp pebbles along the way.

At last, when she was so tired and sore she thought she'd fall down if she tried to go another step, Serjeant stopped in front of a big, fine house, two-storey, with a chimney on its slanted roof. It was painted blue, with a vegetable garden out front and a large barn alongside it.

For all Rachel knew, the blue house could have been Titan's handiwork, one of the places he'd earned his shillings. It calmed her to think of him knocking the nails into the wood, his tall, silent figure moving along the logs, planks, and shingles, his big hands hanging loose till it was time to level off another plank or pummel in the next nail. She stood, sadly hushed, her head drooping, thinking on Titan and trying to soothe herself as the rain streamed off her small, sodden braids and down her cheeks.

Serjeant knocked. There was a rustling within, the sound of people getting ready, and then a man, stern and heavy-set, opened the door.

"I have the slave you asked me to procure for you, Jeremiah Pritchard," Serjeant said without preamble, dragging Rachel in front of him.

"I'm not a slave," exclaimed Rachel. "I'm a free—" Serjeant pinched her arm hard and pushed the cold nose of his gun between her shoulder blades, where the other man couldn't see it.

"That?" Jeremiah managed to look both haughty and doubtful at the same time. "That's the slave you have for me? She's no but a girl."

"Aye, but a fine girl, a strong wench, who'll do your bidding. Brought up in a genteel family, well acquainted with all kinds of housework, definitely of good character. Nothing wrong with her that a bout of hard work won't fix." Serjeant sounded like he was reading off one of the old slave posters. "I bought her off Jonathan Slaggs, Esquire, of Halifax Town. Not because he had no further use for her, you understand, but because he was selling up and journeying to England. She's a slave, fair and square, comes from down south, as you'll hear for yourself if she ever says another word to you."

Although Jeremiah Pritchard didn't reply, Serjeant must have reckoned he'd said enough in the selling way of things, because he kept his mouth clamped while Pritchard clasped his hands together and stood staring at the bare patches of grass out front of the house. Now and then, just to show he was still interested, that he wasn't about to go back in and slam the door, he drew his boot through the mounds of dust, making a wavy pattern. A moment later he'd knock the dust off his boot with a hard stamp. It made Rachel jump the first time he did it.

There were heaps of words that Rachel wanted to say to Jeremiah Pritchard, all of them nasty, or at least pleading, but although Serjeant had withdrawn his gun to hide it from his buyer, she didn't quite dare. Instead she stored them in her brain for later.

Jeremiah harrumphed. Then he coughed. Then he examined her closely, as if she were a mare and he were a horse trader. He squeezed her arms, stared into her eyes, even opened her mouth to count her teeth. She wanted to bite his fingers off, almost died of shame when he touched her. Still, though she loathed him already and was all but certain he could feel the waves of poisonous hatred crashing out of her, he seemed well satisfied.

"Well, they do make the best slaves, the young'uns off those southern plantations. They certainly know how to work their keep. This one's for my wife, so it'll be pleasing if her manners are pretty. What do you want for her? Mind ye, mind ye, watch what you ask. I'm no made of money."

"I was thinking of thirty pounds," suggested Serjeant, fingering his moustache. He sounded uncertain. Even Rachel knew he wouldn't get it.

"Thirty pounds? Are you out of your mind, man?"

"She'd fetch three hundred at New Providence."

"This is no New Providence, as you well know. Listen, I've had a good growing year for potatoes. How about fifteen pounds in money and fifteen bushels of spuds? They'll see you through the winter, no trouble. 'Tis all I have. Take it or leave it."

"And a wheelbarrow," added Serjeant, seeing his chance. "You'll need to give me a wheelbarrow."

"What?"

"To carry all those taters in." Serjeant grinned. His teeth were as black as his brother's.

"Done. Go around the back way. I'll meet you there in a few minutes to settle up. What's her name?"

"Rachel Sparrow," interjected Rachel before Serjeant had a chance to speak.

"Well, Rachel Sparrow, strong and tall, come along in the house and meet your mistress. And try to trail no too much dirt across the wife's nice clean floor. She has the strength for cleaning no longer, and so the more mess you make, the more you'll have to tidy."

"Yessuh," said Rachel. The door closed behind her.

I'm trapped, she thought. *Imprisoned in a house of white massas.*

CHAPTER N°. 5

"You did what?" Eliza Pritchard demanded.

"I gave him fifteen bushels of potatoes, redcoat thief that he is."

"But that's almost all we had stored for the winter. Mr. Pritchard, I despair of you." Eliza Pritchard, Rachel's new missus, went back to her embroidery. A very thin woman, with thin arms, thin face, and thin, straw-like hair, the missus had a greenish, bone-like pallor to her, which made Rachel feel quite sure that she was ill. She was half sitting, half lying in a chair that was almost as long as a bed, and her hands on the piece of fuss-work, as Mamma would have called it, were blue-veined and trembling.

It was hard trying to hate someone who was ill, mighty hard, no matter how Rachel arranged her thinking or tried not to care. Mamma had been ill last year, and Rachel remembered going frantic trying to figure out what would make her better. She wondered if Missus Eliza had the kind of sickness that might heal, as Mamma's had, or whether she would just go on getting sicker till there was nothing left of her.

"I need a cup of water," murmured the missus.

"'Tis what this Nigra's here for. Hey girl, go fetch a drink for your mistress. I'm to the town."

In a second, Jeremiah Pritchard had turned tail and vanished, leaving Rachel and the missus staring at each other. Rachel thought maybe she ought to fetch the water but had no idea where to fetch it from. Besides, she was frozen as a stone. Here she was, in a big dark house that smelled of strangers and sawdust and beef pies, without Titan or Jem or her shawl or the bowl that she ate her cornmeal from. All the dear people and things that made up her life were gone. It was as if she'd been swimming in the cold waters off Cape Roseway and come out of the water to find Birchtown disappeared, and in its place a strange new country that she'd never seen before.

But there was something else, something much worse. Terrible things had happened to her before, but she'd always had Mamma alongside her. She couldn't remember a time when that wasn't the case. Mamma, though she drove Rachel crazy mad with fussing sometimes, was a complete angel. She always knew just the perfect thing to say, though Rachel didn't always understand right away what she was talking about. And she always knew what to do. Now Mamma was gone, maybe forever. And from her last sighting of her, Rachel fathomed that Mamma had been just as scared, just as helpless as Rachel was herself.

"Where's that water?" the mistress asked suddenly. Rachel came to with a shudder, remembering where she was.

"Uh, where should I fetch it from, Missus?" she said at last.

"Never mind that for the moment. Come and stand right here, right in front of me, so I can see you better." Missus looked her up and down. "You're very skinny, your clothes are dirty, your feet are cut and scratched, and you have a big grey stain on your skirt. We'll have to do something about that. Can't have you running around here looking like a beggar. What will respectable people think? Not that it matters too much to me any more."

"That stain'll be from the blueberries. I was collecting them and putting them in my skirt for want of a basket, but I've lost them all now."

"Collecting blueberries? Where do you come from, girl? Who was your master before?"

Rachel swallowed hard. "I didn't have a massa. I'm a free Nigra. I'm not a slave."

"Of course not," said the missus. "We don't have slaves down this way. Or at least we don't say that we do. It's not polite talk. You're a servant, *my* servant now."

It seemed to Rachel that the missus wasn't really listening to her. White folk never did. Nigras could talk and talk till their tongues dried up and fell out of their mouths, but it made no difference. White folk heard only what they wanted to hear or what they said themselves. No Nigra made the slightest dent on their ears. But she reckoned it was worth one more try.

"I live with my Mamma and stepdaddy in Birchtown. I'm not a slave or a servant neither. I'm a free Nigra. I had my certificate of freedom, but Serjeant Gyssop stole it off me." She realized she'd said too much, cringed as though expecting a blow.

But Missus Pritchard only cut a length of purple silk with a tiny pair of scissors, threaded it through a needle, and commenced to sew again. Her hands were so transparent Rachel fancied she could see the veins and bone right through them.

"You'll find the water in a big jug in the back of the house, where we do the cooking. There are cups hanging on the hooks. Bring me a drink, dearie, I'm parched. And then tell me your name—your real name, mind, no fairy stories. Just do as you're told, tell the truth and shame the devil, as they say, and we'll get on very well indeed."

"My name's Rachel, Rachel Sparrow."

"Rachel Sparrow. What a singular name. Are you sure that's it?"

"Yessum. My whole family is called Sparrow except my stepdaddy, Titan. We adopted it as our own on the freedom boat coming here from New York. And Titan says he likes the name well enough and might just take it himself."

The missus was clever enough to ignore the bit about the freedom boat. "Well, if you're a very, very good girl, I may teach you how to write it. Both the Christian name and the last name, Rachel Sparrow."

A missus never taught a slave to read. It was totally unheard of and likely against the law. But if Rachel was shocked, she decided she'd die rather than show it. "I already know how to write my name," she said, marching off with her nose in the air to find the cup.

The missus stared at her in doubt. "I'm not sure this Negro's going to work out," she murmured as she plied her needle. "I'm really not sure at all. She tells such tall tales. Not a *slave*. Lives in *Birchtown* or *Blacktown* or one of those free Negro places. And now she pretends she can *read*. As if she could."

Rachel, on her way to the scullery, heard every word. "R-A-C-H-E-L," she spelled, but too quietly for the missus to overhear. "S-P-A-R-R-O-W. So there!"

It made her feel better for the moment, but then she thought of all the people back home wondering where she was. Titan and Jem (though he was really too little to wonder about anything), Nanna Jacklin and Corey. Soon enough Nathan

Crowley and her friend Ann-Marie would get to hear the news, and they'd be wondering and worrying too. She ached for them all, ached to see and hug them, though she might not dare to hug Nathan. Would they come looking for her? Would they find out where she was?

A big tear rolled down her nose and into her mouth. *Salt,* she thought. *Water. This is just like when the Israelites were slaves in Egypt. Then they crossed the Jordan River and were on their way back to freedom. No matter how bad things are, I have to be brave like them. They got home, and so will I, never mind how much time flows through. Even if I have to wander in the desert for ages and ages.* But there was a pit of loneliness and fear in her belly, and a mountain of doubt in her mind. And Mamma was missing, missing. It was like a chant in her head. *Mamma's missing.* What could be worse than that?

CHAPTER N.º 6

"Missus?" Rachel was dusting the mantel.

"Yes, dearie?"

"Where are we? In which town does this house stand?"

The missus wasn't altogether keen to answer her, not knowing for sure the reason behind the question.

For the first few days she and Rachel had been wary as stray cats of each other. Rachel was scared of the whuppings and hair-pullings that she was sure would arrive soon enough. So far, the missus had been almost too kind. They were nearly the same size, and she'd given Rachel a hardly worn skirt and chemise of her own, with a pair of stout boots besides. But Rachel knew that punishments always came if there were massas and slaves sharing the same house. Titan would say, "That's the way of it, sure enough," and his stepdaughter knew from her own experience that this was true. Although she still felt heartbroken almost to the point of despair, Rachel fetched and carried, she brought water, she scrubbed floors, she slept at the bottom of her missus's bed, and got up in the night whenever needed. She didn't want to feel that tingling slap against her cheek, that pull of the hair that felt like nails driven into her head. She had gotten out of the habit of it.

Meanwhile, the missus had problems of her own with Rachel. She'd never met a slave so hardworking and yet so wicked. Rachel knew how she felt because the missus kept telling her so.

To the missus's mind, Rachel was still uppity as all get-out and told such whoppers of lies her

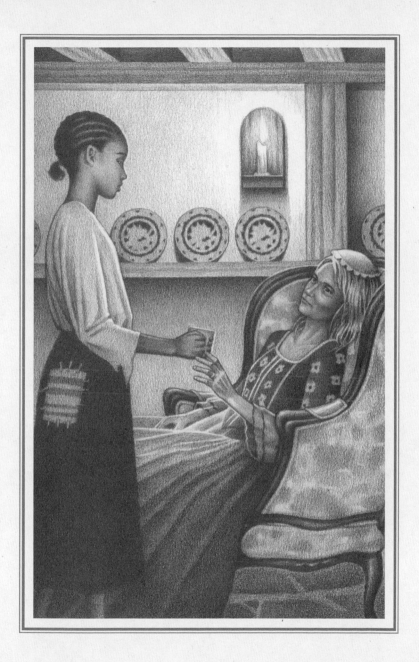

Rachel fetched and carried, she brought water, she scrubbed floors, she slept at the bottom of her missus's bed, and she got up in the night whenever needed.

tongue would likely turn blue and fall off. To save the child's immortal soul, the missus preached to her daily about truth-telling being a surefire way to get to Heaven. "Only good Negroes go to Heaven. There is a special place for them, a kind of Black Town of their own. I must tell you this because it is my Christian duty and I have no desire to shirk it," she said, looking weak as white bread lying there on the sofa.

Rachel pitied her on account of her sickness, but she also thought that white folk were always nagging on about their Christian duty in the most two-faced way. Christian duty this, Christian duty that. Be good. Get saved. And yet their Christian duty allowed them to own a slew of slaves and squeeze all the precious freedom out of them, as if they were ripe red apples fresh picked from the trees. Rachel wanted to tell the missus that, wanted to say that being here was like being squeezed dry and useless as an old apple peel, but she kept her mouth clamped. There were just some kinds of things Nigras didn't say to the whites who owned them. It was too risky by a mile.

Instead she asked again, "Which town are we in? Is this Shelburne? It's a mighty big town indeed, and I don't believe I've ever been down this way before."

"Yes," replied the missus, a little concerned. "This is Shelburne. The east side of it. One day, when you stop telling your monstrous fibs and learn how to be a good servant, I may send you on an errand. I need someone I can trust to come and go for me. As you see, it pleases the Lord to keep me sick, too sick to travel for myself, and you can be sure I reflect upon that often enough."

Shelburne! Close to home! Why, she might even meet up with someone she knew. "I promise never to lie again, Missus," Rachel said solemnly, crossing her fingers behind her back. Sometimes fibbing was the only acceptable truth. "I've been a bad, bad girl. Truth is, I'm a slave, er, that is, a servant, sure enough, and I know my place if ever a Nigra did."

The missus smiled, though the smile was weak and had the touch of death in it.

"Well, I'm glad you're set to be good now, dearie, and that you've seen the error of your ways. I thought you'd come round, given enough time in a kind household. Put my 'broidery away for me, the blue silks and the pink—no, not there, in that drawer with the brass handle—and be careful as can be not to catch the scissors on anything, especially not yourself. Later on, after my rest, if you continue beyond reproach, we'll get out a slate and I'll teach you how to spell your name." Her eyes narrowed. "You don't know, do you?"

"No, Missus, never could make head nor tail of them squiggles." Rachel tried to sound as ignorant as possible. "But I sure would be happy for you to learn me. And I like living here with you. You're a real nice missus, right enough."

The missus gave her a sharp look. Perhaps Rachel was laying it on too thick. She needed to tread carefully. "You go to sleep now, Missus, and

I'll bring you a nice drink of milk in your favourite blue cup when you're rested."

"There's my good girl. There's my very good dearie," murmured the missus. In a minute she was fast asleep.

Rachel tiptoed out of the front room, up the stairs, and into the attic, where she couldn't possibly be heard by anyone, not even the massa if he came home suddenly. Then she jumped almost as high as the roof beams and gave an enormous whoop of joy. That devil Serjeant Gyssop had true enough been walking her round in circles just to confuse her. She was a lot nearer Birchtown than she'd ever have reckoned on. And if she played her cards right, to use the massa's words, she'd be out on the street without a chaperone in no time!

CHAPTER № 7

The massa and missus bickered over Rachel when she was in another room. She could still hear, though. The massa was a harsh man and he would have had her chopping wood, dragging fallen tree trunks away from the property, carrying hefty burdens like a donkey.

"No," the missus insisted. "She's just a girl. You'll use her up."

"She's no but a slave. Slaves are bought to be used up."

"She's a house servant and she does her job more than adequately. I like having her about the place,

I've decided. She keeps me company, and I'm teaching her to read. She's a fast study and is beginning to read to me from my Bible each evening."

"Read, pshaw. You should stop that, 'Liza. You'll be giving her ideas beyond her station. Besides, people will talk."

"I don't have much time on this earth and I'll do what I please, without regard for the neighbours or anyone else except the good Lord. I used to care, but I don't any more. My sickness has made me as fearless as one of God's soldiers. I don't want her wasted on the heavy work, neither. Hire a man for that."

"You've gone plain out of your mind, 'Liza."

"No, I think my sickness has brought me into it. I know what's important now."

"Pshaw," the master said again. He slammed out. Rachel came in.

"Rachel, I can trust you, dearie, can't I?"

"Oh yes, Missus." Rachel bit her lip. She'd been good for a week and was figuring on what would happen now.

"I need you to run an errand into Shelburne for me."

Rachel had guessed right! This was her first, maybe her only chance at freedom. Not that she wanted to lie to the missus or go against her wishes. Not one bit. Much to her own surprise, she found she didn't want to hurt or displease her. After all, Eliza Pritchard, in her sickness and loneliness, grew warmer and more kindly every day. And she stood up for Rachel against the massa. She'd become more like a dear old aunt than a slave owner. But Rachel needed to get herself, or at least a message, home to her family. It was vital to let them know where she was. They were still the important ones. Their sorrow at losing her had to be uppermost in her mind.

"But first of all, thread this needle for me," said the missus. "I can't seem to get the silk through the eye. It's *my* eyes, I'm afraid. They're dimming fast."

Indeed, she seemed to be dimming all over and could barely lift her hand to sew. "Into her last fade," Mamma would have said. "Seein' Heav'n sure enough, but not too much earth, with all them angels flowerin' and flutterin' round her."

CHAPTER N.º 8

An hour later Rachel was on her way, with a basket and directions to the store. It turned out to be the same store that she'd visited with her tuppence when she'd lived in Shelburne in the long gone Maybe House. The store was painted blue, with little diamonds of glass over the door. And there were still the luscious smells of apples and maple sugar. And the barrels of salt fish. And the coils of rope and fishing tackle. And the selfsame horrid lady serving, the one who wrinkled her nose like there was a bad smell under it when Rachel stood in front of her. Oh, how could Rachel have forgotten that? A dozen frightening thoughts came rushing into her head like a hurricane. But dressed in her new chemise and skirt, with her fine leather boots and shiny clean face, Rachel was a heap more respectable than the first time she'd come calling. Just knowing that gave her a lick of confidence.

"Good morning." She smiled. "I'm the servant of Missus Eliza Pritchard."

The woman, who was stacking loaves of bread on the counter, paid no attention to Rachel.

"Good morning," she repeated a little louder, her teeth a mite clenched under her grin. "I'm the servant of—"

"I heard you the first time. Slave you mean, not servant. Right?"

"Yessum." Rachel's shoulders fell. This sure was a miserable woman to deal with. *Odious,* the missus would call her, *odious* and *venomous.* Missus Pritchard knew a trunkful of excellent words, which she unfolded on suitable occasions. Rachel refolded them and packed them back in her own trunk as fast as she could for later remembrance.

"Well, what is it you want? I don't have all day for the likes of you, you know. Spit it out."

"Please'um, my missus says could she have a dozen of the new-picked sour apples as she has the craving for them, a skein of violet silk, and do you have any fabric fit to make me a coat, as winter will be coming on soon? She said to put everything on account, and Massa Pritchard will be in to pay for my buyings directly."

"Humph." The woman plonked down the skein of silk, which she'd pulled from a drawer. Rachel's hand shot out fast and grabbed it as though scared to get a swipe on the knuckles. However, the shopkeeper was already on her way to the back of the store to count out apples, her striped skirt swishing along the floor as she walked.

"Tell your missus there'll be Negro material coming in next week or so that'll make a passable slave coat. I don't have any other fabric at present, except what's good enough for God-fearing white folk."

"Yessum."

"And don't you touch anything else on that counter." Rachel stepped back fast.

The woman returned and filled her basket with the small green fruit. It might be sour, but Rachel's mouth watered all the same.

"Now you get away home, do you hear? And give my best to Mrs. Pritchard. I heard tell she's not a well woman."

"Yessum, thank you." Rachel began to angle towards the door. She moved more and more slowly, like a tortoise without a head, as Mamma would have said. But she was thinking fast. From here she could try to run home to Birchtown. She could find her way well enough through the forest west of the town and around the bay. But no doubt the massa would follow and find her, maybe track her with dogs, bringing a heap of trouble down on the whole family. She'd heard stories of beatings and burnings when slaves had misbehaved, even here. There just had to be another option.

Touching her hand to the doorknob, she took a great gulp of a breath and turned. "There's just one more thing. The missus wants me to run an errand to the Crowley household, and I've forgotten the address."

"You Negro girls haven't the wits of a pigeon. It's on King Street, second-to-last house before the water. Got that?"

"Yessum."

The woman suddenly looked suspicious. "Haven't I seen you somewhere before?"

"No'um. Never." With the apples bobbing up and down, jostling one another and the silk skein in her basket, Rachel fled.

It took all the pluck she had to make her way to Nathan's house, her feet dragging like they had iron chains on them. Once she finally arrived, it took at least a minute for her to get up the courage to knock on the door.

Please let it be Nathan, please, please, she thought as she heard footsteps. But it was Hannah the house slave and not Nathan who appeared. She came out of the house to fetch an armful of chopped wood and stopped dead in her tracks when she saw Rachel standing in front of her.

"They Nigras all searchin' for you," she said, her eyes so round they looked about to pop out of her head. "You and you Mamma. They say mebbe you fall in Port Roseway and wash away into the great sea. My, Rachel, you sure do dress nice nowadays."

"Hannah, I haven't time for this. Listen to me, will you?"

The girl nodded, rather sorrowfully, Rachel thought. No doubt she wanted a chance to chatter.

"Tell Nathan, tell Nathan Crowley, to go down to Birchtown and tell Titan I'm living with the Pritchards out at the east end of Shelburne. Tell Nathan to let Titan know they've taken me as their slave."

"Their slave? They never did."

"Yes, they did, and you must tell. Do you understand?"

"Oh, no, Rachel. It be more than my skin worth to say stories like that to white folk."

"You can, and you must. You hear me? Nathan will thank you for it."

"All right. I try." Hannah looked more sorrowful than ever.

"And tell Nathan to tell Titan that Massa Pritchard's a mighty strict man, and he should be careful. Understand?"

"I guess." Hannah stared at her toes. Then she drew a circle in the earth with her foot, picked up the firewood, and sloped indoors with it.

Could the girl be trusted to speak to Nathan Crowley? Could she even be trusted to remember? Rachel couldn't be sure. And she hadn't a clue whether Nathan would have the pluck to go back into Birchtown with things as they were, the Nigras and the whites having taken so against each other. But there wasn't a skim of time left to waste wondering. She had to get back to the Pritchards with her basket of apples before Missus 'Liza realized something was amiss.

CHAPTER N.º 9

The missus was growing sicker by the day.
And as she grew sicker, she grew even kinder.
She fed Rachel the same food the family ate. She
continued, when not too tired, to teach her how
to read. And she always spoke softly and tenderly to
her. Rachel, despite everything, despite her suspi-
cion of white folk, was coming to love her.
She'd never been treated so fine and fondly by a
white person, not even Nathan Crowley. But
she was afraid for when the missus died. The massa
was stern as a white preacher, and she didn't want
to be left alone with him. He raised his eyebrows

and his voice whenever he saw Rachel and the missus together. And he always spoke to his wife as though Rachel weren't in the room, as if she were a table or a footstool, an unfeeling thing.

"'Tis not fitting you should treat a slave that way. Give her the scraps off our plates and send her to sleep in the barn. The weather's warm enough. She'll no freeze. I'm no for wasting my money, my food, and my fuel on a slave."

The missus spoke very quietly. Every breath was an effort to her. "She prepares our meals and feeds me the very food I need with a spoon. How could I deny her her own share? And I need her by me at night. Dying is a lonely thing, and with you sleeping in your study, she's a great comfort to me. Almost like a daughter, in fact."

"You go mad in your sickness, 'Liza, as I said before. But I'll no interfere. 'Tis said one should humour the sick and no give them more grief than 'tis theirs already." Just then there was a knock on the front door. "Since you need your slave girl with you," he sneered, "best I go answer it."

The massa was not gone a minute when he started to shout. "Get out of here," he was yelling. "And make sure you no come back with your lies. She's my slave fair and square, as Serjeant Gyssop said, and I've had a bill of sale drawn up to prove it."

Neither Rachel nor the mistress could hear a response. They stared at each other in consternation.

"Go, Rachel, and find out what's happening," the missus bade her at last, as the massa started yelling again.

Rachel, her heart pounding, crept to the front door and, crouching behind the massa, saw her own dear Titan, tall and gangly, standing there. So Hannah had told Nathan after all, and Nathan had fetched him. How hard it must have been for them to do what they did, and how brave they both were. Rachel scarce believed it. The sight of her stepdaddy was like taking powerful medicine to cure a sickness.

Titan was no good at talking. He was a strong and silent man whose hands and feet, with their missing toes, worked much harder than his mouth, so he only had a few words to use up every day. But today he kept repeating quietly: "She's not a slave. She's a free Nigra. She's my stepdaughter and I want her back." Rachel had never heard him make such a long speech in her life, and she loved him for it.

"Get!" shouted the massa, raising his hand.

"I'll go to court if need be," Titan threatened.

Nigras never won in court. It was a bad idea and brought all kinds of trouble on their heads— even a murder, once, that Rachel knew of. It was talked of in Birchtown all the time. And, as if everything weren't frightening enough, the massa was now reaching for his long-barreled gun, which stood behind the front door.

In a trice, Rachel knew what she had to do. She rushed between the two men and grabbed Titan's hand. It felt warm and reassuring. How she'd ached for this moment. She'd imagined it a hundred times at night while attending to the missus. How he'd come for her, how she'd return with him, how Mamma would already be back at home, and how they'd all live together once more with Jem. But now, though it almost broke her spirit, she had to send her stepdaddy away.

"Titan," she said, "I'm all right. I can manage. Don't worry your head about me."

"Rachel." He stared at her in astonishment. "You're here. I'll go to court. I'll get you back."

"No. Listen. I want to be with you, you know that. You're my family and I love you more than anything. But the missus is very kind to me, I promise. She's very sick and frightened, too. She needs someone to tend her and I'm all there is. I *have* to stay here."

"Listen to what the girl says. She's no as stupid as I thought," grinned the massa, setting down the gun.

"No, Rachel," cried Titan, totally bewildered. He sounded as if his heart were being torn in half.

"Yes, Titan. Let it be for the moment," she whispered, hoping the massa wouldn't hear what she was about to say next. "When the time comes, when the missus is in Heaven with the angel choirs, as Mamma says, we'll find a way." She let go of his hand and backed away indoors.

"Get!" shouted the massa,
raising his hand at Titan.

"Where is your mamma? Is she with you?" Titan called out after her.

"No. I don't know where Mamma is. I don't know at all." She wanted to add Mamma was enslaved to George Gyssup but was afraid to in front of the massa. He might give her a good whupping. Now she was crying something dreadful. She couldn't believe she'd told Titan to go. She couldn't believe Mamma was still lost. Tears streamed down her cheeks as she stumbled back to the sitting room.

"What on earth is going on out there?" asked the missus, upset herself at the sight of Rachel's tears. Between sobs Rachel managed to tell her.

"So you really aren't a slave," the missus mused. "You were telling the truth all along."

"Yessum. I always tell the truth when I can. Now you can see by my stepdaddy coming after me I was right."

The missus said nothing more, but Rachel could tell she was storing the new knowledge in her mind. Perhaps one day she'd take it out like a mint sixpence, turn it over in her palm, and buy Rachel a whole new life with it.

The missus had grown weak as a kitten.
She couldn't even take gruel from Rachel's
spoon. The doctor came from the town, looked
at her lying there on her sofa, and shook his
head. That was the way of it with doctors. Rachel
remembered from the plantation. They came,
they felt the pulse of their patients, and they
shook their heads. It meant either they didn't
know what was wrong or there was no hope at
all. Usually it meant both.

Micmac medicine was a heap more powerful—it had healed Rachel's own mamma less

than a year back—but she couldn't see these white folks agreeing to swallow any of it. She'd mentioned it to the missus once, but the missus had shaken her head, too, just like the doctor. "Nothing will save me now, child. We must make the best of things as they are."

After the doctor had gone, the missus called the massa in. "Stay where you are, Rachel," she whispered as Rachel turned to go out. "I want you to hear this. Jeremiah, I'm dying."

The massa sighed. "Yes, Eliza, I'm no ignorant of that. I'm sorry for it, I am indeed. You've been a good wife to me, despite your strange fancies. But this is a harsh climate for an Englishwoman."

"I have a dying wish, husband."

The massa sighed again. Dying wishes were sacred. Even Rachel knew that.

"I want you to send Rachel home. I would say I want you to manumit her—free her from slavery—but she's no slave."

The massa put his hands in his pockets and his round face turned red as a harvest moon. "I paid good money for her, Eliza, as you well know, and gave Gyssop all our potatoes for the winter. It'll be harder than ever now to get through the lean season, since the government's reduced our rations."

"All the more reason to let her go. Serjeant Gyssop fooled you, Jeremiah Pritchard. He *fooled* you. No wonder he's never seen about town any more. He plucked the girl from her family, *stole* her, and he sold her where he had no right to."

The massa's hands balled into fists and his face turned more crimson than ever, but he said nothing.

"He sold her *illegally,*" the missus went on, using the long, harsh word to push the truth home.

"Now hang on, Eliza. That's no fair. She's our Nigra, fair and square."

The missus, losing her remaining strength, started to gasp. "She's a free Negro . . . who has cared for me and worked for us . . . for nothing.

You are to give her five guineas . . . for her labour . . . and let her go."

"No!" the massa shouted. He made a move towards Rachel and she cringed, afraid he was about to strike her.

But the missus spoke again. "Listen to me . . . and don't take out your anger and frustration on the girl. She has done nothing wrong . . . It is we who have done wrong."

"This is too much, Eliza. Your sickness has affected your mind."

"You are to give her five guineas . . . Jeremiah . . . and let her go," repeated the missus. "This is my dying wish . . . as God is my witness. Rachel, dearie . . . you've been like a daughter . . . to me . . . my dear. I wish you . . . well."

The massa, not for the first time, stormed out of the room.

CHAPTER N.º 11

It was fall now, a cool, breezy day. Rachel, who had walked all night, feeling her way along the half-familiar path, stood on the crest of a hill, staring down. The last time she'd come by this way, it had been summer. Some of the tall trees were waxing a deep, dark gold, casting their brilliant shadows along the ground. They looked different now she was free again, now she truly understood what freedom meant.

She couldn't see Birchtown yet, couldn't make out the little settlement of Negroes, but she could already smell the wood-fires burning in the stoves and fireplaces and even the pit-cabins below. She knew Titan was down there working, sawing a piece of wood or knocking a nail into their new house. Jem, her tiny brother, was down there too. And Nanna Jacklin, and little Corey, who used to drive her crazy. She couldn't wait to hug him, to hug them all. They were really one big family, and she had come back to them.

Only Mamma was still missing, and that was a great sorrow, but now at least she could tell Titan about Gyssup, and Rachel prayed that when the time came they would find her, too.

She stood for another minute, thinking of Missus Eliza. She had been a good, kind woman. Rachel would carry the memory of her every-where she went, just as if the missus were one of her relations.

The girl walked down the hill slowly, the forest a hazy jumble of shade and sun, a magical quilt of nature. The coat over her arm would keep her warm, the coins in her pouch would see her whole family through the winter. She jingled them softly. The massa had frowned as he counted out every one of them, but in the end he hadn't stinted. He was afeard, he muttered, that his wife would come back to haunt him.

It was time to pick the cranbetties, Rachel thought suddenly, imagining the red, sour berries on her tongue. There had been frost, and they would have come ripe while she was away. Like her adventure with the Pritchards, they were seemingly bitter, but with a curious aftertaste of sweetness.

Still, first things first. She would see to the work of picking tomorrow. In five minutes she would be home.

The massa had frowned as he
counted out every coin, but
in the end he hadn't stinted.

Acknowledgements

Many thanks to my

family and friends;

to Corey Guy, and to Clara and Earnestine of the

Jacklyn family, all descendants of the

original black Loyalists;

to Laird Niven, the archaeologist of the Birchtown site,

and to Patricia Clark of Seneca College, who were both

immensely helpful;

to Leona Trainer, my wonderful agent;

to Barbara Berson and Catherine Marjoribanks,

my terrific editors;

to Cindy Kantor, who brought the idea for

the series to Penguin;

and

to Bookfriends, who are always an amazing source of

support and good humour.

Dear Reader,

Welcome back to the continuing adventures of Our Canadian Girl! It's been another exciting year for the series, with ten girls' stories published and two more on the way! In January you'll meet Keeley, who moves to the newly established town of Frank, Alberta, in 1901, and Millie, a Toronto girl spending the summer of 1914 in the Kawarthas.

So please keep on reading. And do stay in touch. Write to us, log on to our website. We love to hear from you!

Sincerely,
Barbara Berson
Editor

Canada's

1608
Samuel de Champlain establishes the first fortified trading post at Quebec.

1759
The British defeat the French in the Battle of the Plains of Abraham.

1812
The United States declares war against Canada.

1845
The expedition of Sir John Franklin to the Arctic ends when the ship is frozen in the pack ice; the fate of its crew remains a mystery.

1869
Louis Riel leads his Métis followers in the Red River Rebellion.

1871
British Columbia joins Canada.

1755
The British expel the entire French population of Acadia (today's Maritime provinces), sending them into exile.

1776
The 13 Colonies revolt against Britain, and the Loyalists flee to Canada.

1837
Calling for responsible government, the Patriotes, following Louis-Joseph Papineau, rebel in Lower Canada; William Lyon Mackenzie leads the uprising in Upper Canada.

1867
New Brunswick, Nova Scotia and the United Province of Canada come together in Confederation to form the Dominion of Canada.

1870
Manitoba joins Canada. The Northwest Territories become an official territory of Canada.

1784
Rachel

Timeline

1885
At Craigellachie, British Columbia, the last spike is driven to complete the building of the Canadian Pacific Railway.

1898
The Yukon Territory becomes an official territory of Canada.

1914
Britain declares war on Germany, and Canada, because of its ties to Britain, is at war too.

1918
As a result of the Wartime Elections Act, the women of Canada are given the right to vote in federal elections.

1945
World War II ends conclusively with the dropping of atomic bombs on Hiroshima and Nagasaki.

1873
Prince Edward Island joins Canada.

1896
Gold is discovered on Bonanza Creek, a tributary of the Klondike River.

1905
Alberta and Saskatchewan join Canada.

1917
In the Halifax harbour, two ships collide, causing an explosion that leaves more than 1,600 dead and 9,000 injured.

1939
Canada declares war on Germany seven days after war is declared by Britain and France.

1949
Newfoundland, under the leadership of Joey Smallwood, joins Canada.

1897
Emily

1885
Marie-Claire

1918
Penelope